The Hunchback
of Notre Dame

The Hunchback of Notre Dame

by **Victor Hugo**
adapted by **Marc Cerasini**

A STEPPING STONE BOOK™
Random House New York

In memory of Zoraida
—M.C.

www.steppingstonesbooks.com
www.randomhouse.com/kids

Library of Congress Cataloging-in-Publication Data
Cerasini, Marc A., 1952–
The hunchback of Notre Dame / by Victor Hugo ; adapted by Marc Cerasini ;
[cover illustration by Boris Zlotsky].
    p. cm.
"A Stepping Stone book."
SUMMARY: A retelling of the tale, set in medieval Paris, of Quasimodo, the
hunchbacked bellringer of Notre Dame Cathedral, and his struggles to save
the beautiful Gypsy dancer Esmeralda from being unjustly executed.
ISBN 0-679-87429-1 (pbk.) — ISBN 0-679-99437-8 (lib. bdg.)
1. France—History—Medieval period, 987–1515—Juvenile fiction. [1. France—
History—Medieval period, 987–1515—Fiction. 2. Notre-Dame de Paris (Cathedral)—
Fiction. 3. People with disabilities—Fiction. 4. Paris (France)—Fiction.]
I. Hugo, Victor, 1802–1885. Notre-Dame de Paris. II. Title.
PZ7.C3185Hu 2005   [Fic]—dc22   2004019983

Printed in the United States of America   20 19 18 17 16 15 14 13 12 11

Contents

Paris, France
Fifteenth Century

I first saw the hunchback when I was a child. That was long ago, before I became a famous writer.

No one knew my name then. Now everyone in France knows the plays and poems of Pierre Gringoire! Even the King of France has applauded my work. I no longer starve. I am very rich. I live in a large house in Paris and have many servants.

I have told many stories over the years. But there is one story I have never told anyone. It is the story of Quasimodo, the hunchback of Notre Dame.

As I said, I first saw the hunchback when I was a child. It was a bright and sunny morning in Paris. I was rushing to class. As usual, I was late. My chores had taken too long. I was not prepared for the day's studies. I feared my teacher, a young priest named Claude Frollo, would punish me, as he often did.

But as I ran past the huge Cathedral of Notre Dame, my fears were forgotten. I noticed a crowd of people gathered before the church. There was much excited talking. Then the crowd grew silent.

I stopped in my tracks. I stood on my tip-toes, but could not see over the people.

"Take the rags from the child's head!" I heard someone cry from the crowd.

Then I heard the mob gasp in shock and surprise. A young woman screamed and burst from the crowd. Her hand was covering her face as she ran down the street.

The talking grew louder. There were shouts of horror.

What could this marvel be? I wondered to myself. I had to know!

School forgotten, I pushed into the crowd.

I moved closer to the object of everyone's attention. Finally, I broke free of the mob. Then I, too, gasped at the sight before me.

Someone had left a child at the door of the church. This was not an uncommon thing. The people of Paris were poor. Many families could not afford another mouth to feed. Children were left to the charity of the Church.

But this was no ordinary child.

It was a boy, about three or four years old. He was tied to a board with old rags. His face was truly terrible to see. His features were twisted. Red hair topped his misshapen head. His lips were thick, and two teeth stuck out like tusks. One eye was forever closed.

His body was twisted, too. His legs were short, and his spine was bent into a curve. A large hump protruded over one shoulder.

Like a wild thing, the ugly boy struggled against the bonds that held him. He glared at the crowd with hate and fury. Finally, he opened his mouth and screamed.

It was a sound that sent shivers down my spine!

When the child cried out, the mob stepped back in fear. I stepped back, too, then tripped and fell on my rump in the dirty street.

"It's a monster!" one man shouted.

"Aye," said another. "Better to kill it now, for it's a beast from hell!"

The little boy's head twisted from side to side. Then he opened his one pale eye wider and screamed again.

The crowd shuddered in horror. A man dressed in rags picked up a heavy stone from the street and made ready to throw it at the helpless boy.

It was then that a red-robed arm reached out and grabbed the man's hand. The stone dropped to the street. The mob parted.

My teacher, the young priest named Claude Frollo, pushed the man aside and stepped into the center of the circle of people. Frollo was tall and thin, with a bald head that looked like a pink skull.

Frollo stood before the boy and faced down the people.

"No harm shall come to this child," Frollo said in a commanding voice.

"But he is a monster!" a woman cried out.

"God has marked him for his evil!"

"He is only part human," argued a third.

"If he is part human," Frollo replied, "then it is our duty to bring his human side to God."

Claude Frollo passed his cold eye over the crowd of peasants. They were afraid to return his stern gaze.

The people of Paris feared Claude Frollo, and told stories about him. They said he studied the books that a dead sorcerer had left behind—evil books filled with magical spells.

As a child, I believed those tales. After all, Claude Frollo never smiled, and he seldom had a kind word for anyone. In all my life, I only saw him show mercy once. That was on this day, with this poor, deformed child.

"If he is part human," the priest continued, "then that shall be his name!"

Claude Frollo stepped closer to the boy. The child grew silent as the priest placed his hand on that twisted forehead.

"I adopt this child in the name of the Church. From this day forward, his name will be Quasimodo—which means 'part man.'"

Claude Frollo loosened the bonds. He took the twisted child into his arms and held it protectively. The boy called Quasimodo did not cry again. He seemed to understand that Claude Frollo meant him no harm.

Without another word, the priest pushed his way through the crowd and took his adopted son into Notre Dame Cathedral.

And I did not see Quasimodo again for sixteen years.

Chapter 1

The Festival of Fools

Everyone in the city of Paris heard the church bells ringing on the morning of January 6, 1482. This day was a holiday called the Festival of Fools. People all over Europe were excited!

Each country had its own special way to celebrate this grand festival. But the French prided themselves on *their* celebration. They thought it was the best in the world.

People from all over Paris always flocked to the plaza in front of Notre Dame Cathedral. They stood before the bonfire or danced at the Maypole. And every year there was a play at the Palace of Justice.

This year was special because I wrote the play. If my play was a success, I would become famous. But if no one liked it, then I wouldn't even get paid for writing it! I was very nervous. I wanted my play to be perfect.

As it turned out, no one saw my play—and I was never paid for it, either. After all my work, my wonderful play was ignored. All because of a merchant from the city of Ghent.

It seems they celebrate things differently in Ghent! They don't bother with plays. Nor do they have a bonfire or a Maypole. In Ghent, people are less civilized!

Oh, my play *began* as planned. The crowd clapped in delight when the curtains opened and the actors walked onstage. The crowd politely listened to the words I had written.

But suddenly, in the middle of an actor's speech, a loud voice shouted from the crowd.

It was a foreigner—the merchant from Ghent—who rudely interrupted my play. When he shouted, the actors stopped acting. Everybody turned to listen to this man.

"People of Paris," the merchant greeted them. "In Ghent, we don't waste the Festival of Fools watching a silly play."

To my horror, the crowd cheered. I

became angry. My play was certainly *not* silly! I had worked long and hard on it. I was shaking with rage, but the merchant ignored me.

"In Ghent, we know how to have fun!" he told the audience. "We meet in front of the city's largest church. There we elect the King of Fools!"

"And how do you do that?" asked a woman from the crowd.

"Why, we put up a wooden wall with a hole in it. The people who want to be king stick their head through the hole to show everyone their face," explained the man from Ghent.

"And who becomes King of Fools?" the crowd shouted back with interest.

"The ugliest man!" the merchant replied.

"Let's go to Notre Dame Cathedral," a beggar yelled. "We can elect our own King of Fools! Who needs this silly play?"

Soon everyone agreed. The crowd began to leave the great hall.

I had no choice but to join the festival. I, too, would help to crown the King of Fools!

Chapter 2

A King of Fools Is Crowned

The Cathedral of Notre Dame is a huge church made of stone blocks. Notre Dame took years to build and stands in the center of Paris, near the Seine River. The church has huge windows of colored glass and high walls with ornate arches. The tops of those walls are decorated with large stone statues of demons.

These statues, called gargoyles, were placed there to scare away evil spirits and keep the church holy. Their stony faces seemed to be always watching over the people of Paris far below.

Two tall towers filled with bells rise from the cathedral's roof. These bells ring every hour of every day. They call the people of Paris to the church to pray and hear mass.

Every day, Notre Dame is visited by the faithful.

Everything important in Paris takes place at Notre Dame. In the plaza in front of the church, public whippings and executions are held. Speeches are made. Pageants and parades are staged. This is the place where all of the people of Paris, both rich and poor, can meet as one.

The streets of Paris were crowded on the morning of the Festival of Fools. It was a winter day, but the sky was clear and the sun was shining brightly.

Everyone followed the man from Ghent as he led them to Notre Dame. Along the way, more people joined the crowd. Soon all of Paris seemed to be marching with us.

When the crowd reached the cathedral, it filled the plaza.

Never had I seen so many people!

Everyone helped to build a stage. The merchant from Ghent stood in the center of the crowd. He told everyone what to do. Some men brought long wooden boards.

Others brought saws, hammers, and nails. Carpenters began hammering, and soon a wooden wall had been constructed at one end of the plaza.

Two strong men pushed through the crowd. They carried empty wooden barrels. They placed the barrels behind the wall, one on top of the other. An old man brought a ladder, which he leaned against the barrels.

A carpenter hefted a big saw and climbed the ladder. He cut a hole in the wall. The hole was round and just big enough for someone to stick his head through.

The stage was ready.

The merchant from Ghent stepped forward and took his place in front of the wall. Everyone cheered him. He raised his hand, and the crowd got quiet again.

"Anyone who wants to be crowned King of Fools, step forward!" he told the crowd.

Dozens of people moved up to the stage. All were led behind the wall by the merchant. He told them what they must do.

"Everyone must cover their faces and get

in line," he said. "Keep your faces covered until it is time for the people to see you.

"When it is your turn, climb the ladder and stand on the barrels...then stick your head through the hole."

The merchant from Ghent stepped around the wall and addressed the crowd. "You, the people of Paris, will choose the winner!"

The crowd cheered wildly.

"Let the contest begin!" cried the merchant, and then he stepped down from the stage.

When the first man stuck his head through the hole, the crowd clapped halfheartedly. Most agreed he was ugly, but not ugly enough!

The next contestant was not ugly enough either, and the crowd booed him off the stage.

A third man poked his head through the hole. He made a funny face so he looked ugly. No one was fooled by this, and he went away a loser.

Another face popped quickly through the

hole. This man was not ugly at all!

"Get down!" someone in the crowd yelled. "Only your wife thinks you're ugly!"

People laughed at this joke, and the man was booed off the stage.

More people came and went. No one was ugly enough to become the King of Fools, it seemed. The crowd didn't care, because everyone was having fun. Even I was enjoying myself.

"It's the best time of year to be ugly," shouted a man who had already lost. "Being ugly is usually bad. But today you can be king—*if* your face scares enough horses and children!"

Suddenly, the crowd gasped in surprise. A young woman screamed, then the crowd grew silent.

All eyes looked at the hideous face that was poking through the hole in the wall.

A monster had come to the Festival of Fools!

Chapter 3

Quasimodo the Hunchback

I looked up at the stage. A horrible creature was peeking through the hole in the wall. A creature with only one gleaming eye!

Its face was ugly. Perhaps the ugliest I had ever seen. The monster was so horrible that some people turned and ran away. But bolder people leaned forward for a closer look.

"It's Quasimodo, the hunchback," a man in a tall hat shouted.

"It's the mad bell ringer," screamed an old woman. She covered her eyes in fear.

"A monster!" said a pretty young woman in the crowd. "Let me see!"

"It's not a monster," said a handsome young knight named Phoebus. He was wearing shiny armor and sitting on a horse. "That's the hunchback of Notre Dame," the young knight told the crowd.

So this was Quasimodo!

I remembered that day, years ago, when I had first seen the beast that Claude Frollo had named Quasimodo. Though he was horrible then, he was even more horrible now.

"Who is he?" the woman asked the knight.

Phoebus pulled off his helmet and scratched his blond head.

"Quasimodo is the adopted son of Claude Frollo, the archdeacon of Notre Dame," Phoebus answered. "Though he is deaf, he makes the bells sing every day."

"How can a man who cannot hear be a bell ringer?" the man from Ghent asked.

"By the Lord's blessing," Phoebus answered.

"Or curse," said the merchant with a shudder. He could not stop staring at Quasimodo.

Many people listened to what Phoebus said. Most of them had never heard of Quasimodo. They stared at the hunchback.

I stared, too. Never had I seen such a monster.

A tangle of red hair topped Quasimodo's malformed head. His face was twisted, his eyes uneven. One eye was almost closed and was all white, like milk. The other eye was open and stared back at the crowd.

Quasimodo's nose was flat and pushed to one side.

The hunchback's mouth was open and twisted. His two teeth were crooked, like the rest of his face. One tooth stuck out from his jaw like an elephant's tusk. Spit dribbled and dripped from his slack lips.

The people looked at the bell ringer with horror. Some were afraid of him because he was so ugly. But a few people were beginning to cheer and clap.

Then Quasimodo surprised everyone by howling like a dog. His mouth opened and his face twisted even more.

As one, the crowd seemed to understand. That awful howl was his laugh!

When the mob saw Quasimodo's smile, they all began to cheer.

A winner was finally found! Quasimodo,

the hunchback of Notre Dame, was elected the ugliest man in Paris.

He was crowned the King of Fools then and there. The people cheered Quasimodo.

The merchant from Ghent motioned for the bell ringer to climb down the ladder. Quasimodo was too excited to waste time for that. He ignored the ladder and simply jumped down from the barrels.

The merchant went to meet Quasimodo. Other men rushed forward to greet the new King of Fools.

Everyone got a closer look at the hunchback, and the crowd again marveled at his ugliness. Poor Quasimodo's body was as twisted as his face. His head sat between two uneven shoulders. He had no neck. A curved hump grew from his back, like a camel's.

He moved toward the people. His legs were short and bent. Because he was short, Quasimodo walked like an ape. He leaned forward and his hands touched the ground with each step.

His clothes were ragged and dirty, and

they did not fit right. People near him moved away in fear as Quasimodo passed by.

Quasimodo thought his part in the festival was over. He made ready to return to his home in the bell tower. But before he could leave, a poor beggar stopped him. Other beggars came up and took his hand.

The merchant from Ghent had already told the crowd that it was the tradition each year for the beggars to carry the King of Fools through the town. The beggars had even built a special chair for that purpose.

One beggar took Quasimodo's arm. Other beggars set the chair in front of him. But poor Quasimodo was confused. He could not hear, and wondered what they wanted.

Finally, he sat down in the chair. The beggars in their ragged clothes gathered around Quasimodo. Everyone was cheering him, and soon the hunchback began to laugh.

A parchment crown was brought forward and placed on Quasimodo's head. A cape made of many different pieces of cloth was placed over his hump.

Quasimodo kept on laughing when the beggars picked up the chair. The people clapped and danced around him. The beggars carried Quasimodo around the square so that everyone could see and greet the new king.

Only then did Quasimodo know that he was crowned the King of Fools! Quasimodo's heart swelled with pride. He had never been so honored. Quasimodo began to act like a king. He sat on the throne as straight as his crooked back would allow. He pulled the ragged cape over his shoulders and waved to the people.

"Hooray for the King of Fools!" the mob shouted.

The beggars carried Quasimodo through the square, out of the plaza, and through the streets of Paris. The crowd followed with happy cheers.

"Long live the King of Fools!"

"A new King of Fools is crowned!"

"Hooray for Quasimodo! Hooray for the hunchback of Notre Dame!"

Chapter 4

The Dancer and the Archdeacon

I was tired of ugliness. So I did not follow the King of Fools. I knew there was always something to do or see at the festival, and I stayed behind in the plaza.

Many things were happening. There were men and women selling things—clothing and food and even jewels. There were people doing tricks. One man was juggling three stones. There was another man playing a flute. Laughter was everywhere.

Then several young men ran past me. They were students at the university. The men were excited, calling someone's name.

"Esmeralda! Esmeralda!" they cried. "Esmeralda is here! She is dancing by the fountain!"

This sounded interesting!

I followed the young men. I soon heard music and found another crowd of people.

These people were not cheering the King of Fools. Instead, everyone was watching a beautiful young girl dance.

She wore a long skirt of many colors. Ribbons whirled around her as she moved. She shook a tambourine.

"Dance, Esmeralda!" the crowd chanted.

Esmeralda was dancing madly, her long dark hair flying in the wind. I watched her every move. She was graceful and beautiful.

And she was a Gypsy.

Gypsies were people without a home. They traveled from city to city in small groups, called caravans. They were a common sight on the roads of France. Gypsies never lived in one place for very long.

Some people did not like Gypsies. Many people were afraid of them. Even men of the church said Gypsies did the devil's work.

I had never seen a Gypsy before. I had never seen a more beautiful woman, either.

As Esmeralda danced, people threw coins at her feet. Some of the crowd clapped in time to the music she made. Others just watched. Esmeralda danced for a few more minutes. Then she stopped and bowed to the audience. The cheering went on for many minutes.

Quickly Esmeralda put the coins thrown to her in her tambourine. Then she spoke to the people.

"I want you to meet my special friend," Esmeralda said. He voice was as lovely as she was. Then she whistled once. The crowd moved aside and a small gray goat came prancing up to her.

"This is Djali," Esmeralda said to the crowd. "Djali is a very smart goat."

Esmeralda leaned down and whispered into the goat's ear. Then she stood up.

"What time is it, Djali?" she asked.

The goat tapped his front hoof on the street three times.

"Djali says it is three o'clock!"

The crowd gasped. The bells of Notre

Dame had rung three times as Esmeralda was finishing her dance. It really was three o'clock!

"What an amazing goat!" said a student.

"The beast can tell time," said a merchant in the crowd.

"It is a miracle!" a woman cried out.

Then I heard a voice filled with cruelty. It was a voice I remembered from childhood.

"It is the work of the devil!"

Everyone turned to see who spoke. It was a tall man dressed in a long red cloak. His head was bald and his eyes were staring straight at Esmeralda. It was Claude Frollo, the archdeacon of Notre Dame—my old schoolmaster.

Frollo was no longer a simple priest. He had risen to become a powerful man of the Church. Everyone in Paris was afraid of him. He was cruel and did not like Gypsies. His eyes were filled with hatred as he looked at Esmeralda. She shrank back in fear.

"You are a witch!" he shouted, pointing at Esmeralda. "And your goat is a familiar of the devil. The goat speaks to the devil and helps you work your evil magic!"

"No, it is not true!" Esmeralda answered him, with fear in her voice. "Djali is just a goat. He is my friend."

Esmeralda reached down and hugged her pet. Then she looked at everyone in the crowd. No one spoke. They feared the archdeacon, and did not want Frollo to know they had been watching the Gypsy dance.

Esmeralda could see she had no friends here.

"Come, Djali," she said.

With that, the Gypsy girl and her amazing goat left the square. Claude Frollo's eyes followed her as she walked away.

Just then, the Parade of Fools returned to the plaza. The beggars were still carrying Quasimodo. The hunchback was still riding in the chair and laughing.

As the parade neared, Claude Frollo grew very angry. He ran up to the beggars and ordered them to put the chair down.

When Quasimodo saw his foster father, he was ashamed. Claude Frollo had commanded

Quasimodo never to leave the walls of Notre Dame. The archdeacon thought the hunchback was too ugly to be seen by the people.

Quasimodo knew he had done wrong. He had wanted so much to see the Festival of Fools that he had disobeyed the archdeacon.

"What are you doing?" Frollo shouted.

Quasimodo hung his head in fear and shame. Claude Frollo had beaten him before. The archdeacon used a long rope that he kept in his chambers for that very purpose. Now Quasimodo feared he would be whipped right here, in front of all Paris.

"Come here! Now!" Frollo yelled, pointing to the ground in front of him.

Quasimodo could not hear Claude Frollo. But he saw him pointing and he understood. The hunchback moved quickly to obey.

The hunchback leaped off the chair. He pulled the parchment crown from his head and dropped the cloak onto the street. Then the hunchback ran to his foster father, his head bent.

"I...I am sorry," he moaned.

Frollo struck the hunchback across the face with the back of his hand. Then he took Quasimodo by the arm and dragged him away. Off they went toward Notre Dame.

Some people were laughing. Others were sad. The beggars were angry because Frollo had taken away their king.

"What do we do now?" the beggars asked each other. "We have no King of Fools."

"Back to work, then," said one tall beggar to the rest.

With that, the beggars moved away. In minutes, no beggar was in sight.

I shrugged my shoulders. I did not care what happened to the archdeacon or the hunchback. I thought only of Esmeralda.

Never before had I seen someone so beautiful. I wanted her for my sweetheart. I had to find her. I had to see her again.

But Esmeralda was not in the square.

"She is still in Paris," I said to myself. "And if she is here, then I will find her!"

With that, I went off in search of the beautiful Gypsy girl.

Chapter 5

The Hunchback Strikes!

Many hours later, I was still searching for Esmeralda.

It was dark, and the streets of Paris were dangerous. There were robbers everywhere. But still I continued to look for the Gypsy girl.

Once I thought I heard her tambourine. Another time I was sure I saw her dancing for a crowd. Both times I lost her again.

I was about to give up when I saw two men in the shadows. One man was tall and wore a long red robe. The other man was short, crooked, and bent. I knew who they were immediately.

Claude Frollo and Quasimodo.

What were they doing here?

I saw the archdeacon grab the hunchback's

arm. I saw him point at someone across the darkened street. Quasimodo looked. So did I. The archdeacon was pointing at Esmeralda. She was walking with her goat in her arms.

Quasimodo nodded to Frollo. Then the archdeacon hurried away.

The hunchback began to follow Esmeralda down a very dark street. The Gypsy girl had not seen Frollo or the hunchback. She did not know the danger she was suddenly in!

I was afraid for the girl, and did what I had to do. I followed Esmeralda and the hunchback down a grim and dirty alley.

The street was narrow. The walls leaned in from both sides. There was no light. I could hear the squeaks of a thousand rats. I turned a corner and almost slipped in the mud.

Far in front of me, I could see the shape of Quasimodo in the dimness. He still followed the girl. I hurried to catch up to them both before it was too late.

Another turn. This alley was even darker. I could hardly see anything. I put my hand out to feel my way through the blackness. Now I could hear something besides the scurrying of rats. I could hear weird whispers all around me. Shapes rushed past me in the darkness. A hand brushed across my face.

I covered my mouth and tried not to shout out in alarm. Then I heard a woman scream.

It was Esmeralda!

"Esmeralda!" I called in panic. I ran forward blindly. In the dark I tripped on a stone and fell in the mud. I got up and ran again.

"Help me! Help me!" Esmeralda cried.

Now I could see dark shapes ahead—Quasimodo and the Gypsy girl. The hunchback had Esmeralda in his powerful grip. He threw the helpless girl over his back. Djali the goat ran into a corner and bleated in fear.

"Help! Help!" Esmeralda screamed again. The hunchback turned to run away, with the girl still in his grip. I had to stop him!

With a great burst of speed, I finally reached them. I grabbed the hunchback by the arm and pulled with all my might. But he was very strong and easily broke free.

I grabbed him by the leg and held tight.

Quasimodo turned to face me and dropped the girl to the ground.

Now I was staring into the glowing eye of the hunchback. Raising his powerful arms above his head, Quasimodo stepped closer.

Quickly, I made a fist. I hit him once. Then again. The hunchback did not seem to feel my punches. He kept on coming.

The hunchback growled at me like an animal. Frightened, I stepped backward. My foot hit another loose stone. Down I fell, on my back. The wind was knocked out of me.

Quasimodo leaned over me. I could feel his breath on my face as he picked me up. He lifted me high above his head. It was as if I weighed nothing more than a feather!

He bellowed like an ox. He was ready to dash me to the ground! And I was helpless. Every bone in my body would soon be broken.

I was certainly doomed!

Chapter 6

The King's Guards Arrive

I was helpless in the hunchback's powerful grip. I closed my eyes and waited for death. I heard Esmeralda scream and Djali's loud bleating.

Then I heard another noise in the alley. It was the sound of horses' hooves and men shouting.

Suddenly, I felt myself falling. Quasimodo had dropped me as if I were a hot coal. Down I fell, but not hard. Luckily for me, I landed in a soft pile of garbage in the street.

I looked up to see the light from a dozen lanterns filling the alleyway.

I watched as a group of the King's Guards moved quickly toward Quasimodo. All of the soldiers were on horses. Some of them carried lanterns. In the light I could see the hunch-back. He was completely surrounded by these soldiers, but he was still fighting!

One of the men threw a rope around the hunchback.

Quasimodo struggled, but it was useless. Even his strength could not break the rope that was twisted around him. Two of the sol-diers jumped off their horses. They knocked Quasimodo to the ground and tied his hands behind his back.

"We've got him, sir," said one soldier to the leader. I recognized the man who commanded the soldiers. He was the knight named Phoe-bus. He looked down at the hunchback.

"Ho, ho! This is new," laughed Phoebus. "Quasimodo the bell ringer is now stealing women!"

Poor Quasimodo could only moan. He had tried to kill me only a moment ago. But now I felt sorry for the hunchback. Those captured by the guards were often mistreated. Some were never seen again.

Esmeralda ran up to Phoebus and grabbed

the reins of his horse.

"Thank you so much! You saved me from that monster," she told Phoebus. The handsome knight smiled down at her. There was a gleam in his blue eyes. He took her chin in his gloved hand.

"I can see why Quasimodo would want to steal a pretty girl like you," he said to Esmeralda. She blushed in the lantern light.

"Hop up on my horse, girl." Phoebus reached down and took Esmeralda's hand. He lifted the Gypsy girl onto his horse and placed her in front of him on the saddle.

Phoebus called to his men, who were tying up Quasimodo. "Take the bell ringer to the bailiff. He will stand trial for trying to steal this woman."

With that, Phoebus turned his horse and rode out of the alley. Djali bleated once and followed the knight and Esmeralda.

The other guards pulled Quasimodo up off the street and led him away. I watched their lanterns as they walked down the alley. Soon it was dark once more.

No one had even looked twice at me.

I felt as if *I* were the King of Fools.

"What a clumsy hero I am!" I yelled at myself. "Here I rush to save the beautiful Esmeralda, and almost get killed doing it. Then a handsome knight rides up and steals her. They both ride away, while I'm left to sit on a pile of garbage in a dark alley, all alone!"

But unfortunately, I was not alone.

At that moment, grimy hands reached out from the shadows. Men grabbed me. Someone put a sack over my head.

I fought, but there were too many of them.

Hands lifted me out of the dirt.

"Let's take him to the king!" someone muttered. I heard other voices, but could not make out the words.

"Hold him steady," said someone behind me.

I felt a sharp pain on top of my head.

Then blackness—darker than any alley— claimed me.

Chapter 7

The Court of Miracles

I awoke to a living nightmare.

I was lying on the ground and my whole body ached. I reached up and felt a bump on my head. When I heard voices, I sat up and looked around. What I saw was amazing and horrible.

I was in a huge, cave-like chamber. The stone walls were wet and dripping with water. There were many openings in the walls.

Some were tunnels that led into blackness. Others were small shallow indentations with people crowded in them. Fires burned in this huge room. Smoke hung in the air. I could smell food cooking. Dirty children ran past me.

There were hundreds of people here. All

were filthy and wore ragged clothes. More people entered through the tunnels. Most looked crippled, and had canes and crutches.

Lame men limped. Others crawled along the floor, their backs bent. Blind men felt their way along. They carried cups jingling with coins.

Everyone here was a beggar or a thief. It was an entire city of them! In this strange place, deep in the sewers under the city of Paris, the unwanted came at night to live.

I was in the city of beggars!

I had heard stories of such a place. Now I was seeing it with my own eyes.

As the cripples entered the great room, they threw aside their crutches. Men who crawled with twisted backs stood up and walked. The blind opened their eyes and could see.

"It is a miracle," I said, astonished. Then I realized they only pretended to be crippled and blind.

"You are in the Court of Miracles!" boomed a voice behind me. "Here the blind see, the crippled walk. Thieves are kings, and beggars are gentlemen."

I turned to see a fat man in ragged clothes sitting on a huge stone. He held a cup of wine and chewed on a chicken leg. On each side of him stood a strong guard. Each had a sword tucked into his belt.

"When you are in the King's Court, you should bow," stated the fat man.

"I have already seen one king today," I answered bravely. "He was the King of Fools, and I did not bow to him."

"No, but you will bow to me. For I and my people carry the King of Fools on our backs!"

The King of Beggars held out his cup. A young girl ran up and filled it. All the beggars were watching me now. I heard someone laugh.

"What do we do with people who come to our city uninvited?" the king asked his people.

"Hang them!" the people cried as one.

"Just as those above hang us when we come out to beg and steal!" the king continued. "They don't like us on their streets, and we don't like them coming down here!"

The king looked right at me as he ordered his subjects to hang me.

I could not believe it! First I had been beaten up by the King of Fools. Now I was to be hung by the King of Beggars!

Well, I thought to myself, I am a poet and writer—a man of words. Perhaps I should plead for mercy.

"Your Majesty," I said to the king, "I am but a poor beggar myself. I write plays, but I never get paid for them. I, too, am an outcast. The people of Paris don't like me either."

The king gazed at me with new interest. I kept talking. "I want to join you. I want to live here in the Court of Miracles!"

"Oh, so you want to join us?" the king asked me, with a strange gleam in his eyes.

"Yes! Yes!" I answered eagerly.

"You must pass a test," the king warned.

"Anything!" I replied.

"Very well then," said the king with a laugh.

A group of beggars ran up to me. One

placed a small stool at my feet. A rope was lowered from the roof. On that rope hung a stuffed rag doll the size of a man. The doll was covered with hundreds of tiny bells, which jingled as it was lowered.

A beggar took my hand and led me to the stool. "Step up," he ordered me.

I got on the wooden stool, which was very wobbly. "What do I do now?" I asked.

"It is very simple," said the fat King of Beggars. "You must reach into the dummy's pocket and pull out the coins that you find there. You must do that without making the bells ring. If even *one* bell rings, then you will take the dummy's place on the end of that rope."

I swallowed hard in fear. "I understand," I said, and turned toward the stuffed man.

"Please," I said to the dummy, "just keep quiet. My poor life is in your hands." With that, I reached up.

"One more thing," the king said to me. "You must stand on the stool with one foot."

The king and all the beggars laughed.

46

"But that is impossible!" I cried.

"If you do not want to try, then we will hang you now!" the king said, with menace.

"No! No! I-I will try!" I stammered.

"Then good luck, writer," the king said.

I swallowed in fear once more. Then I lifted one foot and balanced on the other. The stool wobbled. I almost fell. I steadied myself and reached out again.

With a loud snap, one of the legs on the stool broke. I fell headlong into the stuffed man. Down I went.

I landed on my rump in the dirt. The bells on the stuffed man jingled loudly. To me they sounded louder than the bells of Notre Dame. These bells were ringing up my death!

The beggars all laughed. Their king laughed the loudest of all. Then he sighed. He turned to the two men at his side.

"Hang him," the king said, and pointed straight at me!

Chapter 8

Saved from the Hangman

Rough hands grabbed me and lifted me off the dirt floor. Two strong beggars held me. Others pulled the stuffed man off the rope.

One man tied the end of the rope into a hangman's noose. Soon I would be deader than the stuffed man!

Everyone was cheering. To the beggars, my suffering was entertainment.

The life of a beggar was very hard. They were treated cruelly by the people of Paris. So in return, they were cruel to everyone who came into their city.

Such thoughts raced through my mind as I made ready to die for the second time that night. My hands were tied behind my back. The noose was placed over my head. I looked pleadingly at the King of Beggars, but he was not looking at me. A fat woman wearing a long skirt was whispering into his ear.

"No, no!" I heard the king tell the woman.

"But you must give him a chance," the woman answered the king. "It is the law. Even beggars and thieves must live by some law!"

"That is true," the king agreed. He turned to the beggars and raised his hands.

Everyone was instantly quiet. Then the king spoke. "The queen has reminded me that we have a tradition here. If any woman wants this man for a husband, he will be spared!"

My heart soared! The men in the room booed. Many of the women cheered. The king looked all around the room.

"Well!" he shouted. "Does any woman here want this man?"

The crowd parted, and three women walked up to me. They all looked at me closely. One woman had a scar on her face. Another had no teeth. The third was very fat and smelled like cheese—old cheese.

The woman with the scar reached up and

opened my mouth. She closed one eye and looked inside.

"His teeth are good!" she proclaimed.

Everyone laughed.

The fat woman poked me in the ribs. "He is too skinny for me!" she said.

"Can you cook?" the woman with no teeth asked me.

"Not very well," I answered.

She stared at me for a minute. "Well, you *do* have good teeth. Maybe you could chew my food for me!"

Everyone laughed at that, but me. Hanging might not be so bad, I thought to myself.

"Well," said the king. "He can't steal from a dummy. He can't cook. And he is too skinny. Doesn't anyone here want this man?"

No woman spoke.

"He is really not that ugly," the king said. "I am beginning to like him. There must be someone here who wants this man!"

Suddenly, I saw a familiar face. It was Esmeralda, with her goat. They were walking toward me.

The crowd moved aside to let her pass.

"Esmeralda!" I shouted. "Don't you know who I am?"

The Gypsy girl stared at me. Did she recognize me? Her goat trotted up to me and rubbed his horns on my legs. Esmeralda looked at me closely. She was deep in thought and did not answer me.

"I was the one who tried to help when the hunchback grabbed you!" I told her. Then she smiled. She remembered me!

Esmeralda pulled her long dark hair back and leaned close to look at me. Her eyes widened.

"Yes," she said at last. "You are the man who tried to save me."

"Yes!" I cried. "Yes! It was I."

"And the hunchback threw you into a pile of garbage," she said. The beggars all laughed long and hard at that.

"Please," I begged her, "rescue me and I will take care of you forever."

Speaking to Esmeralda, the king said, "Do you want him, lass?"

Esmeralda thought for a few seconds. Then she nodded her head.

"Done!" cried the king. "Release him." Suddenly, the beggars began to untie my hands.

"If Esmeralda will have him," the king announced, "then the writer is one of us!"

Everyone cheered at the king's words, though I was sure that some of the beggars would have enjoyed a hanging just as much!

Esmeralda stood at my side, and people began to pat me on the back. "You are one of us now!" they cried. "We stick together and take care of our own."

A group of beggars lifted me on their shoulders. Another group lifted Esmeralda as well. The beggars all cheered louder. We were carried around the huge chamber. Everyone greeted us with smiles.

I had been rescued—for the second time that night!

Chapter 9

Esmeralda Becomes My Bride

People cheered when we were again brought before the king. My head was spinning.

Minutes ago, I was going to be hung. Now I was being greeted like a long-lost member of the family. I smiled and tried to play along.

As Esmeralda and I stood before the king, the Queen of Beggars handed him a broken jug.

"Drink!" he ordered, offering me the jug.

I took the jug from him. It was filled with sweet wine. I put the jug to my lips and drank.

The men cheered. Then the king took the jug from me and turned to Esmeralda.

"Drink!" he ordered her.

She did. And all the women cheered.

The fat woman who thought me too skinny dabbed a tear from her eye. "I always cry at weddings," she said with a sniffle.

"Now," said the king, "you have both tasted wine from the jug. You must make a promise to me and all the beggars who are part of the Court of Miracles."

I nodded my head and Esmeralda nodded hers. Turning to me, the king spoke. "Do you...ah," he stopped. He did not know my name.

"Pierre Gringoire, sire," I told him.

The king continued. "Do you, Pierre Gringoire, promise to take care of Esmeralda?"

"I promise," was my answer.

"Do you promise to protect her?"

"I do."

"Do you promise to share your food with her?" asked the king.

"I do," I replied.

"And to share all that you have with her?"

"I do."

The king asked Esmeralda the same questions. She answered "I do" to each one.

The king lifted the jug above his head. Then he smashed it on the ground. "With this broken jug, I declare you married!"

I felt a tear at my eye. While this was not a legal marriage, it was like a dream come true for me! I had already fallen in love with Esmeralda.

The room roared with cheers. We were taken to sit at a large table. Food was brought in and set down in front of us. There were dishes of cooked chicken and warm loaves of bread. There was rich porridge and cheese. There were even apples.

Even Djali the goat was fed at the table. He loved the porridge!

Everyone was laughing and dancing. I drank wine until my head spun.

That night, the beggars of Paris made merry. And I was one of them!

Better still, Esmeralda was my wife!

Late that night the party ended. Esmeralda, Djali, and I were taken to a tiny room divided by a thick curtain.

"Thank you for saving me," I said to Esmeralda.

She smiled. "You tried to save me."

"You are wonderful!" I told her, then yawned.

She laughed. "You shall sleep here." She pointed to a pile of hay in the corner. "It is Djali's bed, but he will not mind. I will sleep behind the curtain.

"Sleep well, Pierre," she told me. "Tomorrow you must learn to become one of us. Tomorrow you will learn to be a beggar!"

I lay down on the hay and blew out the candle. Then I felt something nudge me. It was Djali. The goat began to snore.

In the darkness I thought about this strange and wonderful day. That very morning I had woken up in my home. I was a writer. I was also alone in the world.

Now I was a beggar. I had no home and slept on a pile of hay. But the most beautiful woman in the world was my wife!

I began to fall asleep. Soon the goat and I were both snoring. I don't know what Djali was dreaming. I only know that I was dreaming of Esmeralda.

Chapter 10

The Trial of Quasimodo

While I found a bride, Quasimodo was being taken to jail. The guards pushed him as they led him to the dungeon. He did not understand why he was being treated badly.

The guards dragged the hunchback to a jail in the Palace of Justice. One guard kicked the hunchback. The others laughed. They threw him into the tiny cell and locked the door.

Quasimodo shook the iron bars of his cell. But even his strength could not break them. He put his head in his hands and began to cry.

Quasimodo did not know what was happening to him. Sometimes the guards talked to him. But he could not hear what they were saying. The sound of the bells had ruined his hearing. Only the archdeacon knew how to talk to Quasimodo.

Why were the guards hurting him? Why had they locked him in a cage?

"I was only doing what I was told," he moaned to himself.

The hunchback was right.

The archdeacon had ordered Quasimodo to bring the girl to him.

"She is a witch and must be punished," the archdeacon had told Quasimodo. The archdeacon was like a father to him. The hunchback always did what the archdeacon told him to do. Why was he being punished for doing as he was told?

Quasimodo pulled at his hair in despair. What would the guards do to him? Would the archdeacon ever find him? Would he ever see his beloved bells again?

These sad thoughts were interrupted by the guards. They came back to his cell to get him. The men grabbed Quasimodo and held him. Though he was stronger than the guards, this time he did not fight. They put chains on his arms and legs. The chains rattled with Quasimodo's every movement. Then they led him through a long hall to a strange room.

The room was filled with books. Quasimodo did not know how to read, but he did know what books were. Even the archdeacon did not have so many books.

Quasimodo saw only one man in the room. The man was old and had a fuzzy gray beard. He wore long black robes and was sitting at a high desk. A large book was in front of him. The book was open and the man was writing in it. He dipped a feather pen into a pot of ink and wrote some more.

The guards brought Quasimodo to the front of the room. He stood before the high desk. The man at the desk was still busy writing. One of the guards spoke.

"Your honor," he said. "We caught this man stealing a woman." At that, the man stopped writing. But he still did not look up.

"He must stand trial," the old man said. His voice was shaky.

"Yes, your honor," the guard replied. The

old man continued to write in his book.

Quasimodo did not know that the old man was the bailiff. Everyone feared him. His job was to enforce the law.

If a man or woman was caught breaking the law, they were taken to the bailiff. A trial would be held. The bailiff would hear the details of the crime and pass judgment. The bailiff made sure that criminals were punished.

Quasimodo did not understand this. No one told him he was on trial. Quasimodo did not even know he had done wrong. This did not matter to the bailiff, who was a cruel man.

Quasimodo stood before the bailiff. Guards stood on both sides of him. He hung his head and stared silently at the floor. The bailiff still did not look at Quasimodo. He just kept writing.

A long time passed before the bailiff spoke.

"Name?" he asked Quasimodo.

Quasimodo did not know the man was speaking to him. He stared at the floor. The bailiff stopped writing, but did not look up.

"Name?" he said again. Quasimodo was

silent. One of the guards poked him and pointed to the old man. The hunchback looked up at the old man. The bailiff began writing again.

"Age?" the bailiff asked.

Quasimodo saw the man's lips move. He thought he was being asked his name.

"Quasimodo!" he said loudly. He smiled up at the bailiff.

The bailiff stopped writing and put down his pen. Finally, he looked down at Quasimodo. His eyes opened wide when he saw the monster standing in front of him.

"What is this ugly creature doing in my court?" the bailiff cried.

"He was trying to steal a woman, your honor," a guard answered.

"A serious crime!" the bailiff said. He stared down at Quasimodo. Then he pointed at the hunchback.

"What do you have to say for yourself?" he asked the hunchback.

Again Quasimodo saw the man's lips move. Again he answered, "Quasimodo!"

Then he continued. "I am Quasimodo, the bell ringer at Notre Dame," he stated proudly. "I am twenty years old!"

The bailiff was very angry. "Why don't you answer my questions?" he shouted.

"I am Quasimodo!" answered the hunchback. "I am the bell ringer at Notre Dame! I am twenty years old!"

The bailiff slammed his book shut.

"Quasimodo the bell ringer," the old man said loudly, "for your crime I sentence you to twenty-five lashes in the public square.

"The whipping will take place in three days," he finished.

But Quasimodo was still confused. He answered in the only way he knew how.

"Quasimodo!" he said. "The bell ringer of Notre Dame! Twenty years old!"

"Why does he say that over and over?" the old man asked the guard.

"He is deaf, your honor," the guard replied.

"Deaf, eh?" the old man said. "I don't like deaf people. For that, he will stay an extra hour on the wheel!"

Chapter 11

The Hunchback Is Whipped

Three days later the streets of Paris were crowded. Everyone rushed to the Cathedral of Notre Dame. They all wanted to watch poor Quasimodo get punished.

All of Paris was talking about how the hunchback had tried to kidnap Esmeralda. Many people came early. They wanted to see the hunchback for themselves. And they wanted a good view of the whipping at noon.

I was there, too. I was working. I was acting like a clown for the crowd. The King of Beggars had taught me this trade.

Now I was Pierre the juggler. I balanced chairs on my head. I juggled three wooden balls at once. The people threw me coins.

I was happy. At least now I was being paid for my work!

Esmeralda was there, too. She danced for the people. She did tricks with her goat, Djali. Everyone loved Esmeralda and her talented pet.

When the clock struck noon, the huge doors of the Palace of Justice opened. The bailiff came out. Behind him guards were dragging Quasimodo, who was still in chains.

For three long days he had waited in his jail. The archdeacon had never come for him.

Quasimodo's head was bowed. His one good eye looked at everyone. The chains were heavy, and he walked slowly. One of the guards pushed him and he fell to the ground. The guards dragged him up again.

The guards led Quasimodo to a large wooden wheel in the center of the square. The wheel was turned on its side, and the men put Quasimodo on top of it. He kneeled as the guards put an iron collar on his neck. His arms were tied behind his back. When they were done, the bailiff stood beside Quasimodo and read from a parchment.

"For the crime of stealing a woman," the old man said in a loud voice, "Quasimodo is to be whipped twenty-five times!"

The people gasped. Twenty-five lashes!

Quasimodo stared at the mob watching him, his head turning left and right. His red hair was wild. His mouth gaped. The people moved closer. Everyone was getting excited now. They wanted to watch the beating.

Then a man in black clothes took the bailiff's place. He was wearing a black hood that covered his face. In his hand he clutched a long leather whip. He snapped the whip. It cracked loudly. The people gasped again.

One of the guards stepped up and tore the shirt off Quasimodo's back. Everyone was shocked to see the large hump that grew from his spine. Poor Quasimodo moaned in fear and shame, but no one could hear him above the noise of the crowd.

Then the man with the black hood spit into both hands and grabbed the whip tightly.

He swung the whip above his head and into the air. He cracked the whip once more and stood over the hunchback.

"Begin the punishment!" the bailiff ordered.

The man in black brought the whip down.

Crack!

The leather whip flashed across Quasimodo's naked back. The hunchback groaned and thrashed. He tried to break free. The chains stopped him.

"One!" the old man yelled.

The whip went back. Then the man in black hit Quasimodo again.

Crack!

"Two!" shouted the old man.

Crack!

"Three!"

The man in black raised his arms many times. Each time the whip struck him, Quasimodo moaned and jerked. Time and time again the whip was raised and brought down. Each time the bailiff counted out loud.

As the punishment proceeded, the people

watching no longer seemed to enjoy it. The crowd slowly grew quiet. Only the sound of the whip and the counting of the bailiff could be heard. That, and the terrible moans of Quasimodo.

Crack!

"Fifteen!"

Crack!

"Sixteen!"

After that, Quasimodo stopped moaning. Again and again, the whip bit into his flesh.

At last, there was a final snap of the whip. The bailiff shouted the number. "Twenty-five!"

The man in black stepped back. He gathered the whip into a loop and walked away. The crowd parted in fear and let him pass.

The bailiff stood next to the wheel and spoke to the people.

"For one hour, Quasimodo the bell ringer will remain here on public display."

A guard handed the old man a sand-filled hourglass. The bailiff turned it, and the sands began to run to the bottom.

"When the sand runs out, the prisoner will

be set free!" the bailiff announced. Then he walked back through the doors to the Palace of Justice.

Quasimodo stayed chained to the wheel. One of the guards threw a bucket of water on his back to wash away the blood. Then two other guards got on either side of the wheel. They began to slowly turn the mighty wheel around and around.

As the wheel turned, everyone could see the terrible wounds on Quasimodo's humped back. But no one cheered. Many people felt sorry for the bell ringer.

Some believed he really had tried to steal a woman. Others thought him innocent. The superstitious believed that because he looked so horrible, Quasimodo must be bad. Many arguments broke out among the people.

"Free him!" some people shouted.

"He is a monster, let him be punished!" others cried.

Quasimodo did not hear them. He just hung his head and turned around and around. More blood seeped from his wounds. Another guard got a bucket of water and threw it on the hunchback.

This second bucket seemed to wake Quasimodo up. He glared at the guard with his one good eye. His lips peeled back in a sneer. Then he stared out at the crowd.

Everyone was startled when Quasimodo lifted his head and shouted.

"Water!" he cried. "Water!"

"The monster is thirsty," one of the guards said. The other guards laughed at Quasimodo's suffering.

"Water!" Quasimodo begged again. The guards just kept laughing. Some of the people watching began to laugh, too.

Suddenly, everyone stopped laughing. A woman with long dark hair had stepped out from the crowd.

It was Esmeralda, with Djali by her side. Her long Gypsy dress blew in the wind. Her dark hair flowed down over her shoulders. Esmeralda went to the fountain and silently filled a pitcher with cold water. As everyone watched, she walked to the wheel.

"Stay back," a guard ordered her.

Esmeralda ignored him. She took the pitcher up to the hunchback and put it to his lips. Quasimodo stared at the Gypsy girl with his single eye. Then he tasted the cool water.

He drank, gulping loudly. Some of the water ran down his chin, but he swallowed most of it. When he was done, he looked down at the girl. He tried to thank her, but the words would not come.

Esmeralda looked into the hunchback's eye and understood. She smiled and reached out and touched his face. Ashamed of his ugliness, the hunchback began to weep. He kissed Esmeralda's hand as tears ran down his cheeks.

No one had ever been kind to Quasimodo before. Because he was ugly and could not hear, people hated and feared him. Now this woman was treating him kindly. Quasimodo's heart was touched by her compassion.

Again he tried to speak.

But another voice spoke up loudly.

Everyone turned to see Claude Frollo, the archdeacon. He was standing with a group of soldiers in armor. The soldiers were led by Phoebus. The crowd drew back in fear of the cruel archdeacon.

"There is the witch!" he shouted, pointing at Esmeralda. "Arrest her!"

Suddenly the soldiers ran at Esmeralda. In fear, she dropped the pitcher and tried to run. But the men in armor were faster. The soldiers grabbed her, and Djali, too. She screamed and struggled as they led her away.

Djali bleated in fear as he and his mistress were dragged to the Palace of Justice.

"Esmeralda!" I shouted.

Quasimodo, too, shouted and tried to break his chains. The soldiers were hurting Esmeralda! But it was hopeless. The chains holding the hunchback were too strong.

Esmeralda screamed once as the soldiers took her away. Then the doors of the Palace of Justice closed behind her.

I tried to rush forward, tried to save my beautiful Esmeralda. But one of the soldiers knocked me down with a club. My head hit the stone street and I knew no more.

Chapter 12

Death or Sanctuary

After his hour on the wheel was over, Quasimodo was finally set free.

The guard removed the chains, and the hunchback jumped down off the wheel. Carefully, Quasimodo picked up his ragged shirt and covered the wounds on his back. Then he ran toward Notre Dame Cathedral.

The people of Paris went back to their homes. The show was over.

For the next few days, Paris was strangely quiet. The bells of Notre Dame did not ring. Quasimodo was too sad to ring them. He just sat high up in the bell tower, watching the people below.

The workmen who fixed the church roof were afraid to go near him. And so he was left alone, to sit next to his favorite gargoyle or in his small stone room in the bell tower.

Quasimodo stayed high above the city. The large stone gargoyles were his only friends. There he sat, from morning to night. His one good eye searched the crowd below. What he was looking for, no one could say.

"The bells have not rung in days," the people said.

"Quasimodo must still be angry about his whipping," others replied.

But Quasimodo was not angry. He was worried. What had happened to Esmeralda? he wondered. Was she safe? Had the soldiers harmed her? He looked for her every day. But he never saw her in the streets below.

At night Quasimodo stayed in his room. He cried for the Gypsy girl and her little goat. He did not know why she did not dance or do tricks with her goat. It was as if the soldiers had removed her from the planet.

The people of Paris did not see Pierre the juggler either. That was because the soldiers had wounded me badly.

A few days after I had been knocked out, I awoke back at the Court of Miracles. I still had a terrible headache from the clubbing.

I learned that some of the beggars had rescued me. A beggar woman had sewn up the cut on my head. Slowly the wound healed.

But my soul was still hurting.

Why had Esmeralda been arrested? What did the archdeacon want with her? By order of the King of Beggars, everyone was trying to find out what had happened to Esmeralda.

The army of beggars listened to every soldier. They spied on all the guards. For many days there was no word.

Then a one-armed beggar came to the Court of Miracles. He whispered something to the king. The king nodded sadly and called me.

"Pierre," he said, "we must speak."

As I listened, he told me what had happened to Esmeralda. With each word my heart froze. The worst had come to pass.

"The archdeacon, Claude Frollo, has proved that Esmeralda is a witch," he told me.

"This is a very serious crime. Witches are hung, or burned alive."

"But Esmeralda is not a witch!" I cried.

"Of course not," the king replied. "But the archdeacon thinks Djali is a magical animal. And that is not all."

"Tell me," I begged.

"Esmeralda has already been sentenced to death. She is to be hung in the square tomorrow. She and the goat will both die."

"No, this cannot be," I moaned. "No!"

"Be brave, Pierre!" the king commanded me. "A beggar's life means nothing. We are not important. Esmeralda will die by order of the archdeacon. We are helpless to stop it!"

The king left me alone. I wept with grief and fury. What could I do?

Esmeralda had saved me from being hung.

But I could not save her.

The next day dawned. I rushed down to the square. The wheel that the hunchback had been whipped on was now gone. In its place, a tall scaffold had been built.

The scaffold had a long flight of steps leading to the top. A man stood there. He was dressed in black and wearing a hood. A shudder ran through me. This was the hangman.

The hangman was busy putting up two long ropes. One for Esmeralda, and one for Djali. At the end of each rope was a noose, ready for their necks!

People were already milling about. In Paris, a crowd always gathered for a whipping or an execution. The people of Paris are cruel, I thought to myself. They all come today to watch my sweetheart die. Just as they came to watch Quasimodo get whipped.

Quasimodo! If it hadn't been for her kindness to the very beast who tried to steal her, then Esmeralda would be safe now. The archdeacon would never have caught her!

These thoughts troubled me as I waited in the square. As the hours passed, the streets became more crowded. People pushed each other to get a better view of the scaffold.

Finally, the clock struck noon. The doors of the Palace of Justice slowly opened.

And there stood Esmeralda, her clothes torn and dirty, her head bowed low. She was thin and pale. She was chained, and two of the guards dragged her between them. Behind Esmeralda was the goat. Djali's guard pulled the stubborn goat along.

Esmeralda was to die, and I could do nothing. Tears ran down my cheeks.

The guards led Esmeralda up the steps and onto the wooden scaffold. The old bailiff was there. He held a parchment in his hands. On that piece of paper were written the words that would doom Esmeralda!

I almost rushed forward at that moment. But a hand on my shoulder stopped me. It was the King of Beggars.

"Hold, Pierre!" he commanded me. "No power on earth can save her."

Across the square from the Palace of Justice, Quasimodo watched from the bell tower. He had been waiting for days. Now at last he saw her. And she was in danger!

The hunchback remembered the pain of

his whipping. Quasimodo knew that the guards meant to hurt Esmeralda. He vowed that the Gypsy girl would not die!

Unseen by the crowd below, the hunchback left the bell tower. He climbed down the wall of Notre Dame. Halfway to the bottom, he grabbed a long rope.

Now he was ready.

Down in the square the old bailiff began reading the proclamation to the people.

"By the laws of France and the Church," he announced, "Esmeralda the witch must be punished." On hearing his words, the people began to murmur among themselves.

"A witch! She's a witch!" they said fearfully.

Everyone was afraid of witches. Being a witch was a serious crime. But not everyone thought Esmeralda was guilty. Some shouted insults at the bailiff.

"You lie!" some shouted. "Set the Gypsy girl free!" they cried. "She is not a witch!" At first, these people made a lot of noise. But when the guards stepped forward and glared at them, they got very quiet. All of them were afraid of being arrested, too!

The bailiff read on.

"Esmeralda has been found guilty of using magic to teach a goat the speech of men," he said.

His next words were like a knife to my heart.

"For the crime of witchcraft, Esmeralda the witch and Djali the goat will hang this day."

With that, the guards brought Esmeralda forward. They pulled her long hair aside and put the noose around her delicate neck. Then they put a smaller noose around the neck of Djali. The goat bleated in fear.

Esmeralda looked out at the people watching her. She lifted her chin up, and looked at the bailiff. Then she spoke.

"Know that you hang an innocent woman! I am *not* a witch."

The bailiff stepped back and pointed at the hooded man in black. "Hang her," he said.

At just that moment, Quasimodo swung down on his rope. He landed next to the bailiff and pushed the old man off the scaffold. Down he fell to the street, far below.

Next, the hunchback turned and kicked the nearest guard. He, too, fell off the scaffold. The last guard saw Quasimodo coming for him and ran in panic down the steps.

Everyone was cheering the hunchback. The hangman rushed forward, swinging a long wooden pole. Quasimodo moved aside as the hangman tried to hit him with the stick. Then Quasimodo grabbed the hangman, who began to scream. He lifted him high above his head and threw him into the crowd below.

People ran away in all directions. The hangman hit the stone street hard.

Quasimodo turned and grabbed Esmeralda. She fainted as he threw her over his humped back and caught the rope again. He leapt into the air and swung out over the crowd. People ducked as he flew over their heads!

Several guards ran at Quasimodo. They carried crossbows. They shot their arrows at the hunchback and Esmeralda. The arrows whizzed by the hunchback and struck the stone church.

Quasimodo let go of the rope and landed by the wall of Notre Dame. Then he began to climb. He carried Esmeralda to the top of the cathedral.

When he got to the roof, he turned and held the Gypsy girl above his head. He began to shout one word over and over again. He shouted it loud enough for all of Paris to hear him.

"Sanctuary!" he yelled. "Sanctuary!"

The people looked up at the hunchback. They were dumbstruck with amazement. Quasimodo had done what no one else could do. He had rescued Esmeralda.

I stood on the ground looking up. The King of Beggars was standing next to me.

"The hunchback is no fool," he said to me. "She is in the church now. There she is safe. The church grants her sanctuary. Even the soldiers of France cannot harm her now."

Safe! Esmeralda was safe. From the hangman. From the guards. Even from the laws of France and the Church.

She was safe from them all. For now.

Chapter 13

In the Lair of the Hunchback

In all the excitement of the rescue, Esmeralda had fainted. When she awoke, she was confused. She remembered a struggle. Then she seemed to be swinging through the air. Was she dead? she wondered. Had the angels carried her away to heaven?

She sat up with a start. She had been lying on a straw bed in a large stone room. A single torch on an iron stand burned brightly. Then Esmeralda saw a shadow fall over her. She knew she was not alone.

Esmeralda turned. She was face-to-face with the monster who had saved her.

Quasimodo crouched in the corner near the torch. His twisted face tried to smile at her. Esmeralda was afraid, but she smiled back.

"It was you who saved me," she said.

Quasimodo turned his head and watched her lips. Esmeralda looked back at him, puzzled. The hunchback put one hand against his ear. "I am deaf," he muttered. "The bells have taken my hearing."

He felt ashamed of his handicap. And his ugliness. He turned his face away from her.

"You don't have to look at me," he said.

But for the first time, Esmeralda could see the truth. She could see that under his deformed flesh, Quasimodo was good and gentle. He was no monster.

Esmeralda rose from the straw bed. Slowly she walked over to the hunchback. He covered his face with his hands.

But Esmeralda reached out and touched his arms gently. Then she pulled his hands down and looked him in the eye.

"Only the blind could think you ugly," she said. "I can see your soul is noble."

Quasimodo could not hear her words. But he understood. He lowered his arms and looked at the beautiful girl. He remembered the question he wanted to ask her.

"Are…are you hungry?" he asked. "I have bread and soup."

Esmeralda smiled. "Oh, yes!" she said.

Quasimodo hurried out of the room. He quickly returned with a large bowl of hot soup. He carried two long loaves of bread, too. He laid the food down at Esmeralda's feet. She sat on the floor and began to eat.

As she ate, Quasimodo talked to her. He told her about Notre Dame—and about his lonely life in the bell tower.

While the hunchback was busy seizing Esmeralda, I was busy, too. I rushed to the top of the scaffold. But I arrived too late to stop Quasimodo from taking Esmeralda.

I had some luck, though. I did manage to rescue poor Djali. I carried the goat from the square in my arms. Djali remembered me and was happy to see me. We sneaked past the guards and went home.

Back at the Court of Miracles, the king called a meeting of all the beggars.

"We must do something to rescue Esmeralda!" the king declared. The beggars cheered.

"But she is safe from the soldiers," I argued. "She has sanctuary in the church."

"But remember, Pierre," the king said, "the archdeacon was the one who had her arrested. He also lives in Notre Dame."

My heart sank. The king was right. Esmeralda was safe from the soldiers of France. She was with Quasimodo. But she was also in the lair of the man who wanted her dead!

"Yes, we must do something!" I cried.

"We will. I have a plan," the king replied. "It is dangerous, but it will work."

After Esmeralda ate her meal, Quasimodo took her to see his tower.

He showed her the bells of the church. Esmeralda was surprised to see how large some of them were. There were many smaller bells all around. But in the center of the tower were the big bells. Those bells were larger than she was!

"I have rung these bells since I was a

child," Quasimodo told her. "They have ruined my ears, but I love them."

Quasimodo was proud of his bells. He jumped on the largest one and rocked it back and forth. Soon the bell began to ring. The sound was very loud. Esmeralda covered her ears. Quasimodo laughed and laughed. He swung back and forth. He jumped from bell to bell. Soon all the bells were ringing.

People ran out into the streets and looked up at the bell tower. The bells had not rung like this since the cathedral was built. Everyone in Paris could hear them. And the sound was full of joy!

Then the hunchback took Esmeralda out onto the balcony. The balcony was very high. At one end a stone gargoyle, as large as Quasimodo himself, stood on the edge of the balcony. It stared with stony eyes.

"This is my friend," he told her. "He cannot speak, and I cannot hear." He patted the statue on its head. Then they both looked down on the city streets far below.

Esmeralda was suddenly very sad. My

whole life is down there, she thought. Will I ever see the Court of Miracles again? Or Pierre? Or little Djali?

Quasimodo watched her as she wondered about her fate. As if reading her thoughts, Quasimodo spoke.

"You must never leave this tower," he said. "If you do, the soldiers will get you. Here, you have sanctuary. Down there, you will die."

Esmeralda began to cry.

"Do not worry!" Quasimodo said. "I will always be here to protect you." But Esmeralda could not stop crying. Quasimodo was sad to see the Gypsy girl cry. He knew she missed her friends. He tried to help as best he could.

"I will always be here," Quasimodo promised her. "You will not be lonely. I will bring you food and drink."

When she did not look at him, Quasimodo reached into his shirt. He pulled out a long wooden whistle.

"Please take this," he told Esmeralda. "I can hear this whistle if it is blown. It is the only sound I *can* hear. If you are ever in danger, use it. I will come."

He placed the whistle in her small hand. Her fingers closed on it. Then Esmeralda turned to Quasimodo. She gazed into his eye. Ashamed, the hunchback turned away.

"I know you love someone else," he said sadly. Then he put his hand on the gargoyle.

"You look at me with pity, because I am ugly," Quasimodo said. "Would you love me if I were not a man? Would you love me if I were a goat? Or a statue made of stone?"

Esmeralda did not answer.

Quasimodo sighed. "If that were so," he said, "I wish I were made of stone!"

With those words, Quasimodo ran from the balcony. Esmeralda watched him leave. Alone, she gazed down at the city below. A tear fell from her eye. Quasimodo is my only friend now, she thought. And I shall live in this tower forever.

She held the whistle close to her breast. Then Esmeralda started to cry again.

Chapter 14

Notre Dame Attacked!

In the days that followed, I grew more worried. The thrill and joy I had felt at seeing Esmeralda's daring rescue was now gone.

Would I ever see my bride again? I wondered. The beggars at the Court of Miracles were worried, too.

One day, the King of Beggars called me to his throne.

"Pierre," he began in a fatherly tone. "As you know, I fear for the life of Esmeralda."

I nodded. Like the king, I knew that the walls of Notre Dame would keep Esmeralda safe from the guards. But it would not be enough to protect her completely.

The king reminded me of the master of Notre Dame. "The archdeacon, Claude Frollo, is her accuser. It is Frollo who had her arrested! She cannot be safe in his church."

I wondered if even Quasimodo could protect Esmeralda from the archdeacon.

The king saw the fear on my face. He smiled and put his hand on my shoulder.

"Never fear, Pierre!" he commanded me. "I have a plan to rescue Esmeralda. It is a dangerous plan, but these are dangerous times."

"What should we do?" I asked him.

"First, we fill the streets of Paris with beggars. We spy on everyone who goes in or out of the cathedral. Then, tonight, we strike!"

"Strike?" I asked. "But how?"

"With an army of beggars!" he said. "Tonight, we will storm Notre Dame."

That night, as the midnight watch patrolled the city, we made ready.

All during the day and evening, beggars had slowly surrounded Notre Dame. They brought with them all the weapons at hand. Some brought torches. Others carried pitchforks. Most had only sharpened sticks. We would be relying on our numbers, not our skill with weapons.

As the hour approached, the king emerged from the shadows. He went to the head of the mob of beggars. With me at his side, he spoke to his army.

"Tonight," he announced, "we rescue one of our own from the evil archdeacon! Tonight, Paris belongs to the beggars!"

The men cheered and lifted their puny weapons. My heart swelled. I was proud to be a part of the Court of Miracles!

"Go now!" the king cried. "And bring Esmeralda safely back to us!"

With one final cry of determination, the army of beggars charged down the street to the church of Notre Dame.

Meanwhile, high above the city, Quasimodo kept his lonely watch over Esmeralda. In the days that had followed the rescue, the hunchback had let no man near the Gypsy girl.

Once, Claude Frollo had climbed the stairs to the bell tower. He had ordered Quasimodo to give the girl to him. For the first time in his life, Quasimodo had defied his adopted father. When Frollo had tried to push past him, Quasimodo had shoved him back down the stairs with a snarl.

Claude Frollo had taken one look into Quasimodo's eye and knew he could not defeat the hunchback. Frollo had left the tower.

The workers fixing the roof of the cathedral had seen Quasimodo's treatment of his master. From then on they continued their work—but they worked far away from the hunchback. They were more afraid of him than ever.

As Quasimodo sat next to his favorite gargoyle, he noticed something strange on the streets below.

Although he could not hear, Quasimodo sensed that all was not right. It was past midnight. He looked down and saw the fires of a hundred torches. They moved through the streets of Paris from many directions. All were coming toward Notre Dame.

Quasimodo jumped down off the walls and ran around the tower. He could see that the church was surrounded by an army of beggars!

Esmeralda stirred from an uneasy sleep. She dreamed that she heard someone calling her name. She sat up on her straw pallet in one corner of the cold stone room.

Yes! She was right. The very walls shook from the sound!

"Esmeralda!" the voices cried. "Esmeralda!"

She rose and hurried across the room. She flung the wooden door open and the sound of a thousand voices filled her ears.

"Esmeralda!" they cried. "Esmeralda!"

"The beggars of Paris have come to rescue me!" she exclaimed. Joy filled her heart. She turned and grabbed her shawl. She pulled the flimsy garment over her shoulders. But when she tried to leave the room, she found Quasimodo barring the way.

"You must let me through!" she cried to the hunchback.

"You must stay!" Quasimodo said. "You are safe *here*, and only here!"

Then he slammed the door and locked it from the outside. Esmeralda pounded on the door, but she was trapped.

"Do not fear," she heard Quasimodo cry through the door. "I shall protect you!"

With that, she heard him shuffle down the hall. Esmeralda pounded and pounded on the door, but he did not return. Soon, she sank to the floor and sobbed helplessly.

Quasimodo rushed to the roof of Notre Dame and looked down. The beggars had totally surrounded the church. Some of them made ready to charge the door. Even the mighty doors of Notre Dame could not hold them back forever!

In despair, Quasimodo searched for a weapon. He looked around until he saw a huge wooden beam the roof workers had been using. He ran to it. With his powerful arms, he lifted the heavy beam and carried it to the edge of the roof.

Below on the streets, the beggars were

shouting and waving their torches. Some of them ran up the steps of the cathedral and pounded on the doors. Others joined them. Soon a thousand hands were pushing on the door. The door began to give way.

"Look out!" a beggar cried suddenly, pointing to the roof. The beggars by the doors looked up, but it was too late. A huge wooden beam came crashing down on top of them.

With screams of pain and fear, the beggars scattered. Some of them were crushed like bugs under the heavy wooden beam. Their moans were heard above the shouts of rage.

"It is the hunchback!" a beggar cried. "He attacks us from the roof!"

All eyes looked up. There, on the edge of the high roof, Quasimodo danced in triumph. He ran back and forth and threw his hands into the air. Quasimodo mocked the crowd from his high tower!

The beggars halted in fear. How could they fight a monster that rained death down on them from above? The king himself ran forward and rallied them.

"The crazy bell ringer did us a favor!" cried the King of Beggars.

Pointing at the wooden beam, he commanded us like a general leading an army. "Pick that up...we shall use it like a battering ram to break the doors of Notre Dame down!"

Another cheer erupted from the beggars, and many men ran to do as he ordered. I made ready to follow, but the king again laid his hand on my shoulder.

"Stay, Pierre!" the king commanded. "I want you to speak to this man."

I turned and saw a humble craftsman. He was one of the men who worked on the roof of Notre Dame by day.

The man leaned close to me and whispered in my ear. "There is another way to the tower," he told me. "There is a ladder in the back of the church. It leads to the roof. Not even the hunchback knows it is there."

"Then lead me to it," I cried.

While I followed the craftsman, the beggar army lifted the beam and used it on the door.

Once, twice, three times the ram battered the door. Still, the doors of the cathedral held.

High above, Quasimodo was desperate. He hefted stones used by the workmen and threw them into the crowd below. Some struck and killed members of the beggar army. But still they came. The beggars were determined to rescue Esmeralda.

The hunchback feared for the life of the Gypsy girl. He had no way of knowing that the beggars were there to save her, not harm her. Quasimodo only knew he wanted Esmeralda to remain in the bell tower.

He wanted her with him forever.

He ran back and forth along the wall. He shouted and screamed in rage and helplessness. Soon the beggars would be through the door!

Then Quasimodo saw a huge cauldron with a flame under it. The cauldron was filled with molten lead. The workmen used the liquid metal to seal the cracks on the roof. But the hunchback saw another use for the hot simmering metal.

Looking around, Quasimodo's good eye followed the grooves in the stone of the roof. These grooves directed rainwater off the roof and into the streets below. Often Quasimodo watched the water flow off the roof, through the mouths of his gargoyles, and down into the streets.

An idea crept into his mind.

With a shout of triumph, Quasimodo grabbed the cauldron and tilted it. The hot metal spilled out. It glowed red in the darkness and sizzled and spat. Gallons of molten lead flowed into the stone grooves and ran like water.

First steam, then melted lead, flowed out of the mouths of a dozen gargoyles scattered along the roof. The hot lead spilled down into the street below.

With a hot splash and a loud sizzle, the first drops of melted metal hit the beggars. There were screams of pain. There were shouts of fear. Many men fell, then burst into flames. Soon flames had spread everywhere. The hot lead rained death down on the beggar army.

They dropped the wooden beam and ran for their lives. The cathedral door remained unbroken. Many soldiers of the beggar army lay on the ground, never to rise again. One of the dead was the King of Beggars himself.

The beggar army was defeated. The survivors fled into the night.

Esmeralda heard the lock on the door click. She jumped up from the straw pallet as the door swung slowly open. She ran to greet Quasimodo. Then she stopped dead. She quaked in fear as a long, red-robed arm reached out and grabbed her by the neck!

"Now you shall die, witch!" Claude Frollo cried as he grabbed the helpless Gypsy girl.

Esmeralda struggled for a moment, but the archdeacon was too strong. She tried to raise the whistle Quasimodo had given her, but Claude Frollo knocked it out of her grip. His bony hands wrapped around her neck and squeezed...

Chapter 15

Together for Eternity

While the beggar army was being attacked, I secretly entered Notre Dame.

I climbed the ladder that the workman had showed me, and then I followed a narrow walkway. Soon I found myself on the roof of the cathedral. I heard the warbling sound of the pigeons that lived on the stone arches.

It was dark. I was alone, but I was determined to rescue Esmeralda.

Far ahead of me, I could hear the sounds of the battle. I heard the cries of fear as the molten lead fell upon my friends. Then the night grew eerily quiet. I wondered what had happened. Had the beggar army finally broken into the church? Or had they somehow been defeated?

I did not know, but I pushed on.

I found a darkened doorway, and went down a long flight of stone stairs. Now I was inside the cathedral. The halls were dimly lit and like a maze. Within minutes, I was lost.

When Quasimodo returned to Esmeralda's chamber, he screamed in rage and fear. The door was open, and Esmeralda was gone!

He looked down and saw that only the whistle he'd given her remained. It was lying on the floor, and the leather strap that had held it around her neck was torn. The wooden whistle was broken.

Quasimodo knew that no beggar had taken the Gypsy girl. He had seen to that. The hunchback knew who'd been here.

While he'd been fighting, Claude Frollo had come and claimed Esmeralda!

With an enraged snarl like a trapped animal, Quasimodo ran down the hallway. He had to find Esmeralda!

Ahead of me in the darkness was a wavering

torch. I peered down the very long, dimly lit hallway. At the other end, I saw a red-robed figure carrying a limp form. Though it was dark and she was far away, I was certain the limp figure was Esmeralda.

With a cry I ran forward. I stumbled down the long hall. Suddenly, the figures I had seen turned off the hallway, and the darkness swallowed them up.

I whimpered in rage and helplessness.

Claude Frollo knew that Quasimodo would never look for him here on the roof!

As the archdeacon tied the long rope into a hangman's noose, he gazed at the still form lying at his feet.

"Yes," the archdeacon muttered to himself, "you are beautiful, witch. But your beauty shall not stop me from doing my duty!"

Quickly, Claude Frollo finished the knot. Then he swung the rope over the neck of a stone gargoyle and tied it tight. Claude Frollo leaned over Esmeralda's still form and placed the noose around her slender neck...

*   *   *

Meanwhile, Quasimodo was frantically looking for Esmeralda. He had run to Claude Frollo's chambers. But the rooms had been empty. He had checked the cathedral, but Frollo had not been there.

Quasimodo was beside himself with fear. He wondered if the archdeacon was taking the Gypsy girl to the king's men.

Suddenly, Quasimodo's eye fell on an empty hook. The hunchback knew what belonged on that hook—a rope. The archdeacon always kept it there. Quasimodo knew this because Frollo often used the rope to beat him.

Now that rope was gone!

Quasimodo rushed from the chamber and ran up the stairs. He had to get back to the roof— before it was too late!

In desperation, I continued my search. I quickly climbed up another dark flight of stairs and ran through a maze of hallways. I feared I would be lost in this cathedral forever.

Finally, ahead of me, I saw a doorway. I felt a cold breeze and knew that the door led to the outside. I pushed the heavy wooden door open and walked out onto a long balcony.

At the far end of the walkway, I saw the red-robed figure of the archdeacon. He was standing stock still. He was looking down over the edge of the roof. His gaze never shifted as I approached him.

"Claude Frollo!" I shouted. "I have come for Esmeralda!"

The archdeacon turned to face me. His eyes were wild. His face was flushed. He shook his head slowly.

"Too late..." the archdeacon muttered. "Too late..."

My eyes followed his gaze. At that moment, my soul died.

There, dangling on the end of a hangman's rope over the streets of Paris, Esmeralda's corpse swung back and forth. The archdeacon had hung her himself!

"*No!*" I screamed and sprang forward.

I rushed to the rope and pulled. In a moment, I held my beloved Esmeralda in my arms. She was already lifeless and cold. As cold as my heart.

Then I sensed movement. I looked up. A loud snarl burst from the darkness. Quasimodo leapt between me and the archdeacon.

"You killed her!" Quasimodo cried in anguish. *"You murdered this gentle woman!"*

Claude Frollo stepped back in fear of the hunchback. But Quasimodo kept coming. No mercy showed in the hunchback's single good eye. And no love for his foster father.

With a mad dash, the hunchback leapt into the air and came down hard on the archdeacon.

There was one loud and final scream as both the archdeacon and Quasimodo, the hunchback of Notre Dame, pitched over the edge of the balcony and into the street, far, far below.

Epilogue

The next day, Esmeralda and Quasimodo were buried in the crypts beneath Notre Dame. No stone marks their graves.

They were laid side by side. The monster and the woman were buried together.

I now knew that Quasimodo had tried in vain to save the woman we both loved. It was only fitting that they be together for eternity.

I returned to the Court of Miracles only one more time. I went to get Djali, the goat. We were alone now, the beast and I. We would have to comfort each other.

It is many years later now. I am rich, and I am famous. The King of France himself reads my stories and poems. I am the most famous writer in all of Europe.

I live in a proud mansion in the center of the city. My companion is an old, gray goat.

Yes, Djali still lives and shares a place at my table as an old friend and honored guest.

My servants are the very beggars who lived through that terrible night. Now they share my fine home with me. The Queen of Beggars, long a widow, is the head of my household staff.

As I said, I am famous for my stories.

But this story—of the woman I loved, and the monster who loved her even more than I—this story has never been told to anyone....until now.

Victor Hugo was born in France in 1802. He started writing when he was very young. He published his first book of poetry when he was only twenty. Later he wrote many plays and novels, including *The Hunchback of Notre Dame* and *Les Misérables*. Hugo's stories are best known for their characters—simple people who overcome great obstacles.

During the 1840s, Hugo became involved in French politics. When Emperor Napoleon III overthrew the government in 1851, Hugo fled France. Although he did not return for almost twenty years, his passion for writing never wavered. Victor Hugo, one of the best romantic writers of his time, died in France in 1885.

Marc Cerasini was born and raised in Pittsburgh, Pennsylvania. He now works as a writer, editor, and screenwriter in New York City. A *New York Times* best-selling author, Mr. Cerasini has written books for both adults and children.

**If you liked this scary story,
you won't want to miss these other
Stepping Stones horror classics!**

Dr. Jekyll
& Mr. Hyde

by **Robert Louis Stevenson**
adapted by **Kate McMullan**

Slowly I poured the white powder into the glass. The red liquid smoked and boiled. There! It was finished. I knew that I might die if I took the drug. But I had to know if it worked!

I lifted the blood-red liquid to my lips and drank it down.

FRANKENSTEIN

by **Mary Shelley**
adapted by **Larry Weinberg**

I had to make other parts of the creature myself. He was going to be big. Eight feet tall! And stronger than any man or woman on earth.

At last I was ready. It was a cold and gloomy night in November. The room was dark when I went in. The creature lay on the table. It was a thing of death. But soon it would have life!

Dracula

BY **BRAM STOKER**
ADAPTED BY **STEPHANIE SPINNER**

That night Jonathan was shaving in his room. He used a small mirror that he had brought from England. There were no mirrors in the castle.

He heard someone behind him. It was the Count. But the Count did not appear in Jonathan's mirror. Jonathan turned white. A terrible thought came to him. The Count was not human!

The Phantom of the Opera

by **Gaston Leroux**
adapted by
Kate McMullan

I crept up a secret passage behind Box Five. I whispered to the managers, "Carlotta is singing tonight to bring down the lights!"

The managers looked around. Who had spoken? Then they looked up. The huge chandelier that hung over the hall was swaying back and forth. Back and forth. Faster and faster. And then . . . Crash! It fell!

"A little present from the Opera Ghost!" I howled.